Rose Iris
and the
Rock Trolls

Rose Iris
and the
Rock Trolls

BARBARA HOPKINS

THE CHOIR PRESS

This edition published in 2021 by The Choir Press

ISBN 978-1-78963-180-7

Contents

Contents

This book is dedicated to Rose Iris Hopkins.

Written by a lady who never grew up but simply grew older. The illustrations are by the author. I would like to thank my husband Barry for his help and patience throughout.

A Visit to Herbie White

Over the next few weeks, Grandmother continued to tell the three girls about Rose Iris. How she would jump out of bed and run straight to the window each morning. She would stare sadly out, hoping to see her dear friends, Leanora, Ilani, or any of the other mud fairies, but they never came past her house. Still, she kept hoping that one day she would meet them again.

She wanted to prove to her mother and father that her adventure had not been a dream. She knew they did not believe her story about what happened to her when she fell into the river. As her clothes shrank in the warm water, she had shrunk with them. Her parents knew she would not lie to them. They thought that she had imagined the whole thing because she had banged her head when falling into the water. It could not have been a dream, of that she was certain, because she still had the enchanted stones, tied with Ilani's plaited, pink fairy hair, tucked safely inside her new golden locket, which she wore around her neck and never took off, not even when she had her bath or went to bed at night.

Rose Iris's mother used to take homemade cakes to an old gentleman called Herbie White. He was called a night watchman, and he slept in a little hut, in the middle of the road, a short distance from their house. Well! he wasn't as old as he looked but he had not shaved for many years, so he looked very old indeed. Outside his hut he had what he called a brazier. It was like a large, iron barrel, with holes in it. There were red hot coals burning inside it, and he used the brazier to boil his very black, sooty kettle.

He was a kindly, happy old gentleman, who always smelt of smoke and coal dust. Although he had a very long beard, he only had small wisps of hair on his smooth, shiny head. He loved to sing, especially funny songs. One particular song was about himself. It made the children laugh so much that he taught them the words. It might seem rude to you, but as he taught them how to sing it, and sang along with them, they sang it anyway. It went like this.

Herbie White, throughout his life, has never yet been shaved,
He'll tell you with a chuckle of the money he has saved.
When it's cold he never wears a muff around his throat,
And in the wintertime, he never needs an overcoat.

Old White's whiskers, old White's whiskers,
The finest sight for miles around.
As he walks along, they sweep the ground,
And once a robin's nest was found, in old White's whiskers.

His cottage is so clean and neat,
And when you walk in from the street,
Since there's no mat you'll wipe your feet,
On old White's whiskers.

Old White's whiskers, old White's whiskers.
When he goes bathing in the sea,
He always brings home shrimps for tea.
One day we counted ninety-three, in old White's whiskers.

My next-door neighbour Farmer Cleggs,
Said, "Bless my soul and down my legs,
Why do my chickens lay their eggs?
In old White's whiskers?"

One day Rose Iris went to see Herbie with her mother but after a while she became bored and decided to return home. Although it was a warm, stuffy day, the sky became suddenly very cloudy, and it started to spit with rain. She hurried along the riverbank, hoping that she would arrive home before the raindrops became larger and fell heavier.

Suddenly there was a flash of lightning. Rose Iris started to count slowly. "One, two, three, four." Then there was a loud clap of thunder. This meant that the storm was only four miles away. Her father had taught her that the best way to know how far away the storm was, was to count the seconds between the flash of lightning and the clap of thunder. She continued counting as she ran as fast as she could, to get home before the storm arrived. "One, two, three." The storm was now only three miles away. Suddenly, she noticed that one of her shoelaces had come undone. So, she stopped running, and bent down to re-tie the lace. As she did so, she lost her balance and fell backwards onto the ground.

"Ouch! Will you please get off my head?" a very cross voice screamed at her.

Rose Iris jumped to her feet and looked at where she had fallen. To her amazement, an extremely angry face stared back at her. It belonged to a large stone, which she had accidently sat on when she had lost her balance.

"Don't you know its rude to sit on someone? How would

you like it if somebody plonked their bottom on your head?" the stone continued.

The little girl was so shocked that she stumbled backwards once more, only this time she quickly stretched out her arm and was able to stop herself from falling onto the ground yet again by resting her hand against a tree which stood right behind her.

"Hey, you. Do you mind taking your fingers out of my eye?" an even angrier voice shouted at her.

When she turned around, she couldn't believe her eyes, for there, staring back at her, from the trunk of the tree, was another even angrier face.

"The trouble with young people these days is they have no manners at all," the tree continued to grumble. "Why, only the other day, two lovers came along this path. The young lad took out a penknife and carved a love heart in my back. Then he cut the letters 𝓑 LOVES 𝓑 in me. It was very painful, and it took ages for me to get over the shock of it."

"I know what you mean," the stone continued sadly. "The day before yesterday, two young boys picked up my smaller friends, one after another and threw them into the river, laughing as they did so. Now I'm all alone, with nobody to talk to."

"I am sorry. I didn't realise stones or trees could speak, or had real thoughts, like humans," Rose Iris replied.

"That's the trouble with human beings. No one considers our feelings," the tree continued to complain. "Why, every morning, somebody brings their dog along this path and has the cheek to let him do a wee on me. How would you like it, if you always had wet, smelly feet? I used to have nice warm, mossy slippers in the winter. Now nothing will grow near my

ROSE IRIS

left foot, and it gets icy cold in the winter. Then my big toe gets sunburned in the summer. Anyway, its most embarrassing when people walk past me and complain that there is a nasty smell nearby. I hope this rain gets heavier so I can take a shower. Of course, tomorrow the dog will wee on me again and make me smelly once more."

"If you would give me time to speak, I would apologise for my lack of consideration, but you are so busy grumbling that I cannot get a word in edgewise," the little girl interrupted. "I am very sorry for sitting on you." She spoke to the stone first. Then she turned to the tree and told him she was sorry for poking her fingers in his eye. "At least now you have met each other and you each have a new friend to speak to".

"Oh! Yes, that's true," said the tree. "Unless, of course, someone throws her in the river, or cuts me down to make something with my precious wood. Like my poor old friend here." As he spoke, he nodded towards a newly carved wooden seat, with the saddest face Rose Iris had ever seen.

"We have a very good plan." A tiny new voice, which belonged to a dandelion, joined the conversation. "When they pick us, we put all white, sticky juice over their fingers. It soaks into their skin and makes them wet the bed at night. That makes their mothers very angry."

"Our plan is even better than that." It was a clump of stinging nettles that interrupted with great glee. "STING them and bring them up in white bumps that ITCH and HURT. They hate it and keep well away from us in the future." They all spoke together and emphasised the words STING, ITCH and HURT, gleefully.

"The only thoughtful human being is Leanora. She wouldn't hurt a flea," the tree interrupted. "I always drop all my dead branches and twigs for her to pick up for her fires."

"Leanora. Do you really know Leanora?" Rose Iris became very excited. She had not met anyone who knew her dear friend, since the old Gypsy woman had helped her to return to her parents, after she had fallen into the river and nearly drowned.

"Of course we know Leanora. Doesn't everyone?" said the tree.

Suddenly, there was a flash of lightning. Rose Iris began to count under her breath. "One, two." The storm was coming closer, it was only two miles away. Then "one", then she had no time to count at all, for the thunder and lightning both happened at the same time. This meant that the storm was now exactly above them.

Her mother had told her never to stand under a tree if there was lightning, so she said goodbye to her new friends, and promised she would never put her bottom on them, or her fingers in their eyes again.

The rain stung her face as she began to run along the riverbank, and it wasn't long before she was soaked to the skin.

That was when she heard the familiar clinking and clattering noise. At the same time there was a soft humming sound, which she recognised immediately. Excitedly, she looked up and was amazed when she saw her dear Gypsy friend, Leanora, approaching along the pathway, with clattering pots and pans on the handle of her pram and looking as soaking wet as she was herself. The little girl ran as fast as her legs would carry her. Throwing her arms around the old woman, she hugged her so tightly that the poor Gypsy could hardly breathe. Last time she had seen Leanora it was impossible to cuddle her, for Rose Iris was as small as a ladybird, whilst the old lady was human sized.

"Where is Ilani?" she asked, when her mud fairy friend did not appear, not even to show off as she usually liked to do.

"Will you please allow me to breathe, child?" the Gypsy struggled to pull herself free from the little girl.

Rose Iris loosened her grip on the old lady and waited patiently for her to answer.

"I haven't seen Ilani for some time," Leanora replied. "She is very busy since she had the children. A boy named Elron and a daughter called Joy. A pretty name for a very sweet little girl. A happy child who is always smiling. Or, at least, was always smiling, until a few moons ago when her father Charles was taken away by the rock trolls. Ilani is terribly sad because she cannot leave the children to try to rescue him."

"I wish I could help," Rose Iris said sadly.

"Well, you might have been able to come with me, if only you still had the three enchanted stones." The old woman looked sadly at the little girl.

"Oh! But I do. You see, I was so upset when I had to leave my grandmother's silver locket with Sala, in exchange for the Marble Stone, that my mother bought me a new locket. It is made of real gold and I keep the Black Stone, the Hollow Stone and the Marble Stone, tied with Ilani's hair, safely inside. When I came back to the human world I almost lost them, for they were no larger than three tiny pieces of grit. Now I keep them safely inside my new locket, and have them tucked away out of sight, behind the collar of my dress. I can't come with you though, because I would not like to worry my parents again, if I do not return as usual from Herbie White's hut."

"You needn't worry about your mother and father," Leanora replied. "Have you forgotten that when you returned to the human world before time had almost stood still here? When I returned you to your world last time only a few minutes had passed since you fell into the river, whilst you spent many days in the magical world, searching for the enchanted stones. You will have to take the stones from your locket and give them to me. Remember, they were larger in the other world. Much too big to keep in a small locket. If you do not remove them, they will cause your pretty necklace to burst as it shrinks."

The little girl did not question the chances of her not returning safely. She opened the locket to reveal the enchanted stones and marvelled at the beautiful, pink strands of Ilani's hair, which held them tightly together. She removed them with the tips of her fingers and put them carefully into the old Gypsy's hand. They were so tiny that she thought she might drop them. If they fell onto the ground, she would never be able to find them because they would mix with all the other stones and grit that covered the path.

"I'm ready, Leanora. Please will you work your spell to take me to the magical world?"

Leanora put the stones carefully inside the little tin that she had used to keep them in last time Rose Iris visited the world of magic. It had the word "Cashews," printed on the lid.

"You must touch the stones and I will say the magic words." She smiled in a kindly way as she spoke. Then she placed her hand gently on the little girl's shoulder and began to work her magic spell.

"Delgora, delgora, esparto, ventura.

Malafont, gorgana alamantura."

She repeated these words several times as she had before, when she had brought the little girl back to her human world, from the magical world. Then she replaced the lid of the tin and popped it carefully into one of the pockets of her tattered blue cardigan, before giving it a gentle tap.

The rain ceased to fall, and the sun began to shine down warmly. The little girl's hair started to dry. Then her clothes began to shrink as they also dried in the sun. The heat caused them to release warm steam and they began to feel tighter and tighter, as they became smaller and smaller. Then, suddenly, she felt herself getting tinier and tinier as she began to shrink with them. After a short while, she was no larger than the beetle that passed by and wished her a very good day. He was so beautiful, as the sun shone on his back and reflected all the lovely colours that gleamed from the droplets of water that shone on his wings.

It felt a little odd being small again. She was used to seeing for a long distance, whereas now she could not even see above the blades of grass. Once more, Leanora towered high above her. She was not alarmed, however, for she had been here before.

Leanora stooped over and rested her large, weather-worn hand palm upwards on the grass, allowing Rose Iris to climb up and sit on the end of the old Gypsy's plump forefinger. Then she steadied the tiny girl with her thumb, before carrying her carefully and placing her gently in the pram, on top of the old blanket. This brought back memories of her previous visit to this other world, and she remembered her reason for wanting to become small again. "Poor Ilani, who now has two children to care for, and poor Charles who has been taken away by the rock trolls," she thought.

"The mud fairies have had to move from their beautiful home by the river." Deep frown lines formed on the old Gypsy's forehead as she spoke. "Those horrible rock trolls have been poking about in the bushes, and behind stones, looking for the mud fairies and other creatures who shelter amongst them. Once they find their hiding places, they take prisoners back to their troll kingdom. They only take the menfolk; the women and children are of no use to them at all. Men are strong and able to work in the ruby mines, which lay deep below the rock trolls' world."

"Their Queen, Elvira, is evil and wants to rule all who live in the settlements around her kingdom. Using the rubies, she will be able to buy an army. She knows that the people who fight in her army will be wicked, even to think of attacking innocent people for rubies. These are just the sort of rogues that she is looking for. The poor mud fairies only want to live in peace and are not prepared for war. Neither are the earth crabbits, the wind whistlers or the rock doppies," she continued.

"So where are the mud fairies living now?" The little girl was afraid for the safety of her friends.

"I don't know," the old woman replied. "They are always moving because they cannot allow the Queen's men to find them. If they were found, goodness knows what may befall them. The last I heard, they were forced to move from one muddy puddle to another. Only the womenfolk, children and the old people are left. Once the men are taken to the rock trolls' world, they are never seen again. Thank goodness for the rain we are having. At least there will be plenty of muddy puddles for the mud fairies who remain to bathe in, or they might all die."

"What can I do to help my friends, Leanora? We will have to plan the best way to save them." Rose Iris was extremely afraid for the safety of the mud fairies.

"Charles, Edan and Kire, together with almost all the male members of the many different tribes that inhabit this world, are being held as prisoners by Elvira," Leanora replied. "We have to get someone into the palace and find the dungeons to release them. There is one person who may be able to help us. I am on my way to meet Toddy the fox right now. He has an army and I am sure he will be able to help us."

Toddy the Fox

So, they travelled for several days, until finally, they came to an open field covered in grass, poppies and the odd stalk of golden, ripe corn. Many tall trees and thick bushes grew along the ditches that bordered and enclosed the field.

Suddenly, from the undergrowth, there crept a sly old fox. He looked enormous to the little girl, but she wasn't alarmed, he did not frighten her, since Leanora had the enchanted stones in her pocket and she knew anything could happen whenever the old Gypsy was close by.

"Rose Iris, meet Toddy." The old Gypsy woman started to stroke the fox as she spoke. "Toddy, this is Rose Iris, she is a human child."

The fox scratched his ear, then he scratched his bottom, before finally rubbing the top of his nose and scratching his bottom again. "Pleased to meet you, my dear." He nodded towards the little girl as he spoke, in a very posh and rather snooty voice. Then he continued to scratch himself all over.

"I am happy to meet you too, sir," she replied. She liked his handsome face and his lovely red hair, but she thought he was a little smelly. Then she strained her neck to look behind him, since his army was nowhere to be seen. "Maybe he has left them behind and will order them to follow later," she thought.

"Are you prepared? Do you have your army with you?" Leanora asked.

"Yes, but we will not be able to defeat the trolls without a crafty scheme." He was very good at being sly and crafty and

TODDY THE FOX

had already thought of an extremely good plan. "I have more than a hundred soldiers. If we are clever, we will be able to free the prisoners and hopefully overthrow Queen Elvira," he replied. "I will summon my two captains, and we will discuss the best strategy." So, he threw back his head and made the weirdest howling sound.

Suddenly, his hair started to stand on end, it waved from side to side and gradually a parting began to form over the top of his head and down to his snout. Then, two little heads popped out. One wore a tatty top hat, whilst the second had on his head a beautiful cavalier's hat, decorated with fine feathers. They looked carefully around, before crawling along the strands of hair, along the fox's snout and plonking themselves down on the tip of his very wet nose. They balanced there, with their legs dangling and swinging. Rose Iris saw that they were animal fleas and realised that the reason for Toddies scratch-scratch-scratching was because the flees were biting him, so he was itch-itch-itching.

"This is Captain Dandy and Captain Snooty." The fox introduced the two officers. "It's about time they did some-thing useful. All they do is bite me and cause me to itch all day. If I could, I would shake them off, but they cling too tightly."

"Toddy has a plan which we believe to be very good," Captain Snooty rose to his feet. Captain Dandy stood also, and it was easy to see that they were very good friends, since they put their arms about each other's shoulders in a jovial way.

"It's Queen Elvira's birthday soon. You must make a present, Leanora. Make it look pretty and tie a big bow around it. Elvira will find it hard to resist," Captain Dandy said.

"I can't see how a pretty package will help. Have you gone mad? Giving the Queen presents will not make her change her mind about making all the surrounding kingdoms her own." Leanora could not believe what she was hearing.

"No, of course not, but before you tie up the present, we and our army will be safely positioned inside," Captain Dandy interrupted.

Leanora thought for a while. She was so deep in thought that she bit her bottom lip and made it bleed. "I think that your plan might just work," she said. Then she thought deeper. "Oh no, it is much too dangerous. We will have to think of another plan." Then she thought even deeper. "Well! it may work, but I cannot let you enter the troll kingdom under this plan alone." She sat down on the grass, after checking there were no stones that she might put her bottom on and thought for a very long time. At first there was a serious frown on her tanned face. Then, gradually, the frown changed to a glowing smile.

"I have the perfect solution," she said. "I will make a magic potion. It will be difficult, because I will have to obtain a handful of water maidens' tears, some natter from a natter-jack toad, some pollen from a bee's knees, and finally, some moondust. This will make a powerful sleeping potion. While Rose Iris and I search for the people who may help us collect these ingredients, you must find the mud fairies, the rock doppies, the wind whistlers and the earth crabbits. Get as many other creatures as you can find, then meet us by the entrance to the trolls' kingdom." The old lady was very pleased with their plan.

"Oh no! Leanora, please don't allow Toddy to find the mud fairies, he may eat them." Rose Iris was concerned for her dear friend Ilani and all the other mud fairies.

The fox, however, was equally concerned. "How could you suggest that I am capable of eating poor little mud fairies? I insist on an apology." Toddy felt most insulted.

Captain Snooty and Captain Dandy were also shocked. They could not believe that she had made such an unkind remark.

"Don't worry, Rose Iris, your friends will be completely safe with Toddy," Leanora assured the little girl.

"In that case, I apologise for my rudeness." She thought she saw tears in his eyes as she looked up at him. "I really didn't mean to be unkind," she said.

Leanora built a fire, and they all sat and discussed the plan. Captain Snooty and Captain Dandy, together with a third flee, sheltered under a mushroom. Toddy sat at Leanora's side. He smiled as she gently stroked his back, and soon he was fast asleep. The smile stayed on his face as he began to snore rather noisily.

"Tell me more about Captain Snooty and Captain Dandy, Leanora," Rose Iris asked.

Leanora knew the little girl would ask this question, so she was ready to answer with a little poem she had made up.

"Captain Snooty, is not an ordinary flea.
He was born on a mouse in the palace, you see.
So, blessed with pure royal blood was he,
And living a life of complete luxury.

Until, one day, our gracious Queen,
Screamed in horror, for she had seen,
The poor little mouse, who was not very clean,
On her table and stealing a haricot bean.

The shocked royal children all started to wail,
Prince Charles tried to catch the mouse by his tail,
As it ran up the wall, to the curtain rail,
Looking terribly scared, and extremely pale.

Then he slid down the curtain, till he reached the floor,
And as fast as he could, he made for the door.
But his little heart pounding he stopped running, for,
Completely exhausted, he could run no more.

A horrible man, who was short and fat,
Tried hard to catch him but slipped on the mat.
As he fell on his bum, and flattened his hat,
The children just giggled and said, 'fancy that'.

A second man, who was tall and thin,
Came running towards him, amidst the din.
The mouse made for the kitchen, and once within,
Hid safe and sound, in the food-waste bin."

"So, what happened to the mouse?" Rose Iris was most concerned for the poor little creature.

"Well, you know what happens to your food waste, dear. It goes to the rubbish tip of course. So, the mouse lived quite happily on the rubbish and Captain Snooty lived contentedly on the mouse, until the day the captain saw Toddy the fox, sifting through the rubbish. That was when he decided to move home. He left the mouse, who had never been happier, and took up residence on my dear friend.

"Captain Dandy was born on farmer Brown's cat. He always wanted to be an adventurer and travel the world. He has lived on a camel in the desert, a koala bear in Australia, and a lion in Africa. The lion was brought to England to live in a zoo, but Captain Dandy did not like living in there, so he hitched a ride on a rat called Rumpy, who happened to be very friendly with Toddy.

"Toddy often visits the rubbish tip at night, especially when he is very hungry, and sometimes he meets his friend Rumpy. There is usually plenty of food on the dump, so they do not have to fight each other for the scraps that are thrown away. When Captain Dandy saw Toddy's beautiful, thick fur, he thought it was much nicer than Rumpy's and so he moved home once more."

"The two captains seem to be the greatest of friends, Leanora," the little girl chimed in.

"Oh yes, they are, but there is one problem which has recently become very awkward. You see, Captain Snooty is in love with a sweet little lady flea called Colleen, and it is causing some problems with their friendship, because Captain Dandy is in love with the same little flea. As you can see, they are both flirting with her under that mushroom. Colleen is enjoying their attention and refuses to say which one she prefers," the old Gypsy replied. "Now it's your bedtime, for we have to make an early start tomorrow."

CAPTAIN DANDY, COLLEEN AND CAPTAIN SNOOTY

Maranina and Mr Natterson

Rose Iris awoke to the very pleasing scent of burning wood as it floated silently through the air, and finally crept under the hood of the old pram where she had been sleeping. Every now and then a loud, sharp cracking sound broke the silence, and she realised that this was the sound from Leanora's fire. Then her ears picked up the old Gypsy's gentle humming. Surprised to notice that it was still quite dark, she blinked her eyelids a few times and yawned sleepily, before arching her back and stretching out her arms and legs as far as they possibly could stretch to wake herself up. Suddenly she heard an awful creepy voice calling.

"Whoo goes there, whooo? Whoo goes there, whooo?" She jumped up and looked around, but she saw nobody.

"Whoo goes there, whooo?" Once again, the voice called eerily.

It seemed to be coming from high above her. Rose Iris looked up into the trees and was surprised to see, sat up on one of the highest branches, a large brown owl. She was very afraid.

"What if he is hungry and wants to eat me?" she thought, but before she had time to call Leanora, the voice called again.

"Whoo goes there, whooo?"

"Don't be afraid, Igywanna-the-Wise. It's only Leanora and her friend, Rose Iris," the old Gypsy called up to the owl.

"Ooh. Yoo tis yooo. Yoo tis yooo," the owl continued in his creepy voice.

IGYWANNA-THE-WISE

22

Leanora was pleased to see the little girl had woken up. There was so much to do and so little time to do it in.

"Ah! At last, you are awake, I thought you were going to sleep forever. We have to make an early start, for today we must collect some of the ingredients for my magic potion." Leanora was sat on her blanket, with a warm cup of tea in one hand and a long stick, to which she had attached a metal fork, in the other hand. On the end of the fork there dangled, over the fire, a slice of bread. Suddenly, the old Gypsy reached forward, just in time to stop the bread from falling off the fork and into the fire. She broke off a tiny crumb of the black, smoky bread and passed it to the little girl.

"Leanora, I have been wondering! How are we going to get the maidens' tears without hurting them and making them cry?" Rose Iris did not want to hurt anyone.

"Oh, that will not be a problem. You see, every morning at dawn, before the sun is fully risen, water maidens cry for all the sad and lonely people in the world. All the poor and hungry, or sick," the old woman replied. "There is a gently flowing stream nearby, and they will be easy to find there, but we must hurry or we will be too late, and they will no longer be crying."

So, after they finished eating, they set out with all the pots and pans once more jingling and jangling on the old pram. Leanora was not concerned about the noise, for the water maidens would recognise the sound and know who was approaching, and nobody was afraid of the old Gypsy.

Before long they arrived at the banks of a stream. All was silent. Nothing stirred, not even the dragonflies, who needed the warm sun to heat up their cold bodies before they were able to fly.

The glow from the sun was just beginning to rise in the distance, but the river still lay covered in an eerie mist, which floated softly and silently like a ghostly, grey sheet over the water. Leanora laid out her blanket on the ground and sat silently on the bank. Rose Iris also sat silently on the old Gypsy's hat, atop of her head. After a while, there began a soft sobbing sound, which filled the air about them. Then, suddenly, came a loud splash and movement in the water, followed by a terrible wailing sound, which floated all around them.

"Leanora, I think a very big fish has just jumped out of the water," the little girl whispered excitedly.

"Shh! no dear, it wasn't a fish. Can you see, on that rock over there, by the blossoming tree? It is a water maiden," the old Gypsy replied. She strained her eyes to identify which maiden she saw. Eventually she recognised that it was Maranina.

Rose Iris squinted and peered through the swirling mist, but she saw nothing, until suddenly, a slight movement and a break in the gloom revealed a wonderful vision. She could not believe what her eyes beheld. The most beautiful creature, half human and half fish. Her green hair was just distinguishable through the ghostly vapour drops. The lovely creature continually sobbed and wailed eerily.

The old Gypsy took off her shoes, socks, and trousers. Then she rolled up her skirt and tucked it into her knicker-legs. She tried not to disturb the water as she waded into the stream very slowly, so as not to startle the sad creature as she approached her.

"Maranina, don't be afraid, it is only I, Leanora," she whispered.

MARANINA

The maiden stopped crying, only long enough to nod an acknowledgement to the old lady, before once more continuing her sad, haunting wail.

"I'm sorry for your sadness, dear. Please don't think me heartless, but I require some water maiden's tears to make a magic potion. Could you spare me some of yours?" Leanora drew a little closer as she spoke.

To Rose Iris's amazement Maranina cried into her cupped hand and held out the crystal-clear liquid towards the old Gypsy. She did not speak. She could not speak, for she could not stop crying long enough to do so.

Leanora took from her pocket a tiny bottle and held it out to the water maiden, who carefully allowed the contents of her cupped hand to trickle into the bottle. The old lady put a cork in the top to prevent losing any tears and thanked Maranina for her help. The sun was now beginning to climb higher above them and almost instantly Maranina ceased wailing. Gradually, a warm smile began to form across her beautiful face. She blew Leanora a kiss and with a flash of her silvery, green tail, she was gone.

The little girl wasn't sure if she had been real, or if she had imagined the whole thing. When she looked at Leanora, however, she still held the little bottle tightly in her hand, and so Rose Iris knew that it hadn't been a dream.

The old Gypsy tucked the tiny bottle into her pocket and stepped out of the water. She dried her wet feet and legs with a piece of old rag before pulling her skirt out from where she had tucked it in her knickers. Afterwards, she replaced her trousers, socks, and shoes.

By this time, the dragonflies and butterflies had awoken from their nightly sleep. The sun shone high above and

Leanora was concerned that if they did not hurry, they would lose the chance of collecting the next ingredient for her potion.

As Rose Iris waited for Leanora to prepare for their next adventure, there was a loud splash and, before she knew what was happening, she landed face down in the mud. Something hard hit her on the head and something cold and sticky landed on the back of her neck. No matter how she struggled, she was unable to get up. It took all her strength to pull her face from the mud. Then, after straining her neck, she managed to look up and over her shoulder. She was surprised to see that sitting with his foot on her back was a very large, ugly toad.

"Yuck, get off," she shouted, as she struggled to free herself. The toad took no notice and if it weren't for Leanora, she would never have been able to shake him off. "Yuck, you're really blinking slimy," she shouted, as the old lady lifted the toad off her and stood him gently on the grass. "Flipping heck, can't you look where you're going." She continued to scold the toad as she smoothed down her dress and wiped her muddy face with her handkerchief. The toad ignored her tantrum and said nothing. That was all he had to say to her.

"Aah, just the gentleman we were hoping to find. We didn't have to look far, Mr Natterson, since it seems you have found us instead. I must say, you are looking very handsome and smart today." Leanora was as surprised to see the toad as Rose Iris, although she was not as angry. "I'm concocting a magic potion and need some rasping natter from a nattering natter-jack. It's lucky you came along."

"It wasn't very lucky for me," Rose Iris sulked. She glared

MR. NATTERSON

at the clumsy creature. She did not think him handsome, or smart. She thought he looked like a circus tent. He was dressed in a red and yellow striped jacket, a yellow waistcoat, brown trousers and a boater hat. She did, however, admire his beautiful black and white shoes. What had hit her on the head was the walking stick that he carried.

The toad continued to ignore her tantrum. "Well I don't usually natter at this time of year, my friend, but as it is you who requires my help, I will do my best to oblige. Who is your rude little friend?"

"I'm not the rude one. It was you who jumped on top of me and made me all muddy." As she spoke, she used Leanora's old rag to wipe her face. "You should be ashamed of yourself."

"Now, now, Rose Iris. Stop making such a fuss. I'm sure Mr Natterson would not put his foot on you if he had known you were there." Leanora was not used to seeing the little girl so angry.

The toad completely ignored her. He began to puff out his throat, but when he opened his mouth, no sound came out. He tried again. Still there was silence. "It's no use, you see I only natter in the spring, when I am looking for a lady friend. At this time of year, they are not interested in me, so I simply don't waste my time." He tried once more and puffed up his throat so full of air that the little girl thought he would burst. Then it happened. A rasping croak escaped and echoed along the bank of the stream. He puffed up again. Leanora waited with the open bottle, to catch the sound as it escaped from his mouth. As soon as the noise entered the bottle, she quickly replaced the lid so as not to lose any natter.

"Thank you, sir. I'm sorry to have put you to so much

trouble, though I am very grateful for your help. It was very lucky that you passed our way. What a lot of time we will save, not having to look for you," she said. "Well, we must be on our way, for I have some more items to collect for my potion. Thank you once more." So, they continued on their way, with an occasional raspy croak echoing behind them.

"Don't you think Mister Natterson is a rather ugly fellow, Leanora?" the little girl asked.

"Certainly not, child. In toad circles, Mr Natterson is considered to be very handsome. I am sure toads would find you to be extremely ugly, but they would not be so unkind as to say so. Anyway, UGLY IS, AS UGLY DOES," the old Gypsy replied.

Rose Iris did not understand. "What do you mean UGLY IS, AS UGLY DOES?" she asked.

"Well, a person can be what you may consider ugly, but only do kind things, so they are really beautiful. On the other hand, someone you think beautiful may be unkind to others. These are the really ugly people. Now we must collect some pollen from the bee's knees, so we will need to find some flowers, and I know just the place." Leanora looked sternly down at the little girl. "You really must try not to throw tantrums, dear."

Rose Iris did not argue, for she knew Leanora was quite right. There was one thing that puzzled her though, and she knew the old Gypsy would know the answer.

"Leanora, why do some animals wear clothes and others don't?" she asked.

"Oh, that's easy to answer. Those as loves them, wear them, and those as hates them, refuse to wear them," her friend replied.

William's Garden

They travelled along a smooth path, which ran along the outskirts of a forest. The trees stood still since there was not even a breeze. Their branches were covered in leaves of many different shades of green. Flowers covered the ground and wherever the light could shine through the trees, grass, moss and mushrooms were growing thickly below. Dragonflies and butterflies danced from one leaf to another, and birds sang their many different songs. Squirrels leaped along the branches and once a shy deer crept nervously out from behind a tree.

"This must be the most beautiful place in the whole world," the little girl said. "I wish I lived here."

After some time, they arrived at their destination: a pretty garden that surrounded a quaint little black and white cottage with a rambling rose trailing around the front door. The garden was filled with wonderful flowers and heavenly scents.

Leanora walked up the long front path to the door of the cottage and made a gentle rat-a-tat sound with the knocker.

After a short while, there came a shuffling noise and a puffing sound. The door opened to reveal a kindly looking old gentleman. He had a very flushed pink face covered in fluffy, sparse, white whiskers. Rose Iris thought his face resembled a ripe peach. He wore a checked dressing gown and brown leather slippers.

"Hello, William, I was passing by and wondered, could I sit in your garden for a while?" The Gypsy knew he would not refuse.

He looked pleased to see her, but he did not see the little girl who peeped out from under the old felt hat, for his eyesight was not as good as it used to be. "Leanora, you know you are always welcome. If you sit on the old iron seat, under the apple tree, I'll bring you a nice cup of tea and a chocolate biscuit," he said.

As he turned to walk back into the house, there was a very rude noise, which Rose Iris suspected was a puff of wind, which had escaped from his bottom.

Leanora walked around the side of the house and into the back garden. She found the old iron seat and sat contentedly breathing in the lovely flower scents that filled the garden.

She placed her old felt hat, containing Rose Iris, on the seat beside her and enjoyed the soft fresh air that floated about her head and through her unkempt hair.

It wasn't long before they heard the old man's slippers shuffling and scraping along the gravel path. There was the sound of cups and saucers as they rattled on the wooden tray that he carried, and every now and then there was the same popping noise, which Rose Iris was sure was him blowing off. The old man and Leanora seemed not to notice, and so she tried to ignore it. This, however, was not easy, and she found it very hard not to giggle. When William sat down for a chat, the old Gypsy moved the little girl under her hat, so that there was no chance of him spotting her. Now Rose Iris could not see him, but she could still hear him letting wind occasionally. The old Gypsy passed her a tiny crumb of biscuit. It tasted delicious, especially the chocolate covering, which was quickly melting in the sunshine.

Leanora and William chatted for a short time before the old man said goodbye. He shuffled back up the garden path

LEANORA

WILLIAM AND FRIENDS

to the cottage, the empty cups and saucers rattling on the tray as he went.

Leanora reached into her pocket and pulled out a handful of corn seeds. She sprinkled them on the ground and called, "There's pickings for all. There's pickings for all."

Suddenly, a wood pigeon came swooping towards them at such a speed that he crashed headlong into one of William's empty flowerpots, breaking it and scattering broken bits of pottery everywhere. He started to gobble up the corn immediately.

"Hello Bert. This is Rose Iris," the old Gypsy introduced them to each other.

"How are you, Mr Pigeon? If you like you can call me Rosie, that's what my parents call me," the little girl said.

"My tooe bleeeeds, Ro-sie. My tooe bleeeeds, Ros-ie," He held out his right foot, and sure enough his poor little toe was covered in blood.

"I'm very sorry to hear about your toe, Bert, but I hope it will get better soon. You must have cut it on the broken flowerpot," Rose Iris replied. She took out her handkerchief and gently wiped away the blood, but the cut continued to bleed.

Soon all the seeds were gone. "Well, if you have no more seeds to put down, Leanora, I'll be on my way. I get hungry very quickly, did you know?" As Bert flew away into the distance, they could still here him calling. "My tooe bleeeeds, Ro-sie. My tooe bleeeeds, Ros-ie. My tooe bleeeeds, Ro-sie. My tooe bleeeeds."

The bees busily buzzed from one flower to another and as they did so the pollen from the flowers stuck to their legs. Leanora spoke to one of them as it landed nearby.

"Mrs Bee, I wonder if you would be so kind as to allow me

BERT

to take just a tiny amount of your beautiful yellow pollen, for a magic potion I am making?"

"Of course, I can spare some pollen. I will just have to work a little longer to replace it, but since it is for you that will not be a problem," the bee replied in a buzzy voice.

The Gypsy took the tiny bottle from her pocket and removed the cork. The bee then stood on the neck of the bottle. Once there, Mrs Bee gently tapped her legs on the glass and two bags of fluffy, yellow pollen dropped silently inside. Leanora replaced the cork, and the bee resumed her work, buzzing happily as she did so.

After a short while the old Gypsy noticed that the sundial nearby was throwing a shadow, which suggested that it was ten o'clock. "We will never get back to where we have to meet Toddy. We cannot laze all day in this garden, enjoying ourselves," she said.

"Do you have all you need for your potion now, Leanora?" Rose Iris asked. She was looking forward to returning to the beautiful forest that they had passed by earlier.

"No dear, there is just one more thing to collect and I cannot get that until it is dark. So, we will start our journey back the way we came. I will be able to collect what I need tonight once the sun has gone down," the old Gypsy replied.

So, they left the garden and started their return journey. Rose Iris clung to the blanket under the hood of the old pram, laughing excitedly each time it bounced over the uneven path. If she had not held on very tightly, she would surely have been thrown out of the pram and onto the ground.

MRS BEE

Petrina the Witch

It wasn't long before they arrived back at the forest that Rose Iris loved so much. As they approached, Leanora suddenly stopped pushing the pram, and stood open-mouthed.

"Oh! No. How terrible, it's Petrina," she cried.

Both the old Gypsy and the little girl were amazed to see the sight before them. The beautiful green forest, with the sound of songbirds, and animals creeping quietly amongst the undergrowth had gone. In its place they saw an ugly sight. Every tree had died and stood petrified. The ground, instead of being covered in grass, moss and mushrooms, was now covered in brown, golloping mud, which gulped and bubbled continuously. The dead roots of trees protruded from the mud and all was silent, except for the odd glubbing sound, as the stinking mud smouldered. There were no birds, no butterflies or dragonflies, and not a single furry animal to be seen. The air was filled with a terrible rotting, stinking smell.

"Whatever has happened Leanora?" Rose Iris could not believe what she was seeing.

"It's that evil witch, Petrina. Why must she destroy every-thing?" Leanora was used to seeing destruction whenever or wherever Petrina had passed by. "She has petrified the forest. No matter, I will soon change it back," she said.

"Oh, no you won't." There was a loud screeching voice followed by a spooky, high-pitched cackle. Then suddenly, a dark, shadowy figure appeared from behind a dead tree.

Rose Iris realised it was a witch, for she was dressed all in black and sat on a broomstick. On the broomstick behind the witch sat her pet, a pink cat, and on the front, a frog danced happily.

"I will," said Leanora. She took from her sleeve a long wiggly stick. Rose Iris realised that it was a magic wand when the old Gypsy pointed it towards the forest. "Mortica grandii," she whispered.

Immediately, the trees began to come alive. Tiny new leaves began to sprout on their branches. The mud ceased to bubble, and grass and moss started to grow on the ground.

"No, you will not. Escrato piranti," Petrina screeched as she waved her own wand. Immediately, the new baby leaves shrivelled and died. Then she turned her wand towards her pink cat. "Ilio preferlio purple," she screeched. There was a silver light, which went from the end of the wand and whistled towards the cat. In an instant, the cat changed from pink to purple. A small brown bat that accompanied the witch kept dodging the wand. He hated the idea of becoming purple or pink.

Leanora directed her wand towards Petrina. "Voloman discarto," she shouted. A blue light flew from her wand and hit Petrina on her enormous nose. This made the evil witch lose her balance. She fell off her broomstick and was only able to grab hold with one hand, in order to stop the broomstick from flying away from her. The broomstick headed towards the ground, and Petrina could not see where it was taking her, for she was back to front, and could not turn around. She tucked her legs up as high as she could, because she did not want to be swallowed by the mud. Then she spotted Rose Iris, who was sat on the edge of Leanora's hat.

PETRINA THE WITCH

"Ilio preferlio green," she screamed. The silver light once more left the end of her wand. This time, it whizzed through the air and hit the little girl. Rose Iris screamed in horror, as she saw herself turn from her natural colour, to bright green.

"Valcato ignato," Leanora screamed as she directed her wand towards Petrina once more. This caused the witch to sink lower and lower, and no matter how high she tried to lift herself up, she gradually slid screeching and cackling, until she disappeared into the gulping, gurgling, golloping mud, and completely vanished from this story.

"Mortica grandii," once more Leanora spoke the magic words.

Slowly the trees became brown again. They reached out their branches towards the sky. New green leaves began to squeeze themselves from the branches, then slowly they opened out and stretched themselves as far as they could to enjoy the lovely, new fresh air as it moved about them. The golluping, stinking, black mud ceased to bubble, and gradually the grass began to grow once more. Moss and mushrooms hid in the shadowy corners, birds sang their beautiful songs, dragonflies and butterflies flitted about, and the squirrels and deer crept carefully out into the open. Once more the forest looked the same as it had when they passed by earlier that day.

There was just one thing that had not been put right. Poor Rose Iris was as green as the grass.

Leanora began to laugh. "I quite like you that colour. Maybe I will keep you like this," she said with a giggle.

"Oh no, please put me back to my usual colour. I hate being green," the little girl begged.

"Of course. I was only joking." The old Gypsy pointed her wand at the little green girl and said, "Ilio preferlio, your skin as it was." Instantly Rose Iris returned to her natural shade.

"I say. You there. Excuse me, but would you like to share supper with me?" It was a soft, kindly voice that spoke.

Rose Iris turned to look behind her and was surprised to see a bank vole, sitting upon the branch of a bush that was covered in delicious-looking berries. He looked very large for a bank vole, but he wasn't really. It was because she herself was so tiny.

"Are you speaking to me?" the little girl replied.

"Yes you, the one with the two tails," he said. "I would be happy to share my supper if you would like. There's plenty here for you and me, and I would like some company. Someone to speak to for a while. By the way, my name is Bramble Bottom."

"I'm Rose Iris. I'll have to ask my friend Leanora if it is safe to eat those berries. You see, children should never eat wild fruit unless their parents tell them it is safe to do so. Why are you saying I have two tails? I don't even have one tail," said the little girl. She looked behind her. Maybe Petrina had given her a tail, as well as turning her green. She was relieved when no tail was visible.

"Yes, you do. I can see them both, hanging from your head," replied the vole.

"Oh, they aren't tails, they're plaits." She was so relieved when she realised what her new friend had seen. "Although, I must admit, sometimes boys pull them, and call them pigtails."

"Ugh, how horrible to have two pigs' tails, hanging from

43

BRAMBLE BOTTOM

your head. Pigs are rather smelly, dirty animals, I hope you aren't smelly too, because you do look a little dirty. I would rather not share my food with you if you are smelly." The vole was beginning to wish that he never invited the little girl to eat with him.

"Of course, I'm not smelly. I am a little dirty though. You see, a large toad called Mr Natterson put his foot on me, and made me fall face down in the mud. I haven't been able to wash properly since, because I have been very busy helping my friend." Rose Iris turned to Leanora. "Will it be alright for me to eat the berries?" she asked.

Leanora knew which berries they were and told her she could eat them. Then she reminded her never to eat anything wild, unless a grown up told her it was safe to do so.

"Don't eat the red ones," said Bramble Bottom. "They are very sour, and don't eat the green ones or you'll get a tummy ache. Your friend can have some too if she wishes."

So Leanora, the vole and the little girl enjoyed a tasty supper.

Moonbeams & Moondust

There was no time to waste. They continued to travel until they arrived back at the stream, where they had met Maranina and Mr Natterson. By this time, it was beginning to get dark. Leanora built a small fire. She filled her kettle in the nearby stream and placed it on the fire to boil. Then she toasted some bread, and they sat and chatted while they ate it. Suddenly there was the sound of laughter and happy, chattering voices. Rose Iris was amazed to see a large leaf floating along in the stream. It was not the leaf alone that interested her. It was the four people who sat laughing happily inside it, as it floated gently over the water. Each of them looked almost identical to the others. Each had a pair of turquoise wings, covered in a lemony dust, which shone in the moonlight. They all had pale yellow, shortly cropped hair and wore no clothes at all.

When they saw Leanora sitting on the bank, they became extremely excited. Still laughing and chattering, they guided the leaf boat to the bank of the stream, and all four jumped out and onto the damp mud. They seemed to glow with a lemony light that fell like dust from their wings. Still chattering happily, they approached the old Gypsy. Rose Iris could see the amazement in their eyes when they saw her and she realised that it was probably because they had never seen such a tiny human being before.

One of them spoke in a high-pitched voice. "Hello, Leanora, it's good to see you again. Who is your new friend?" she asked.

"Oh, this is not a new friend. I have known her for some time now. Her name is Rose Iris," the Gypsy replied.

The four people all ran up to the little girl and one of them introduced herself and each of her companions. "I am Dawn, and my friends are Dusk, Eve and Morn, we are moonbeams. Would you like to come in our boat and float down the river for a while?"

Rose Iris turned to Leanora. "Do you think I should?" she asked. "It looks like it would be great fun, but the boat will be dreadfully overcrowded and may sink under the water."

"That's alright," Eve spoke. "I will stay behind and watch, whilst you take my place in the boat."

The little girl thought it was most kind of the moonbeam to stay behind, whilst she took her place to enjoy floating along in the moonlight. Eve flew up to a branch in a nearby tree and watched as Dawn, Dusk and Morn helped the little girl into the boat. Rose Iris was a little afraid that she would tip the boat over when she first climbed in, but before long she was as excited as the others, as they floated happily along the river. The only sound to be heard was the chattering and laughter of the three moonbeams and one little human as they guided the boat with their fingers and feet. Eve remained on the branch watching her friends, and Leanora kept a watchful eye on Rose Iris from the bank.

They stayed playing for hours and did not notice that the darkness of night was beginning to fade. Dawn suddenly realised how late it was.

"Oh dear, we were having such fun that we haven't noticed how quickly the time has passed. Doesn't time go quickly when we are enjoying ourselves?" she laughed. "We must hurry back to the moon before daylight comes, or we will all melt into the sunshine. We will have to go now." Still laughing and chattering, they returned to the bank to say goodbye to Leanora.

Rose Iris wished that they could play for longer, but she realised that her new friends had to leave before sunrise.

"Can I ask just one favour of you before you go?" The old Gypsy felt into her pocket and pulled out her little bottle, containing all the magic ingredients she had already collected.

"Do you have time to leave me just a small amount of moondust? I need it for a magic potion I am making."

DAWN, DUSK, EVE AND MORN

48

They were happy to help, and each one flitted carefully over the bottle, whilst shaking their wings. Soft, lemony coloured powder gently floated down and into the bottle. Leanora replaced the stopper quickly, as she had with all her previous gifts. She looked very pleased with herself.

"That is the final ingredient," she said. "Now you must hurry back to the moon before the daylight arrives. I would not like you to melt into the sunshine because you stayed too long to help me."

As they left, and flew still laughing and chattering, back up towards the moon, each little person blew Rose Iris a powdery, lemony kiss, which floated silently and softly down to cover the little girl in the magic dust. She watched the pale turquoise glow of moonbeam wings as they faded further and further into the distance, before finally disappearing completely from sight.

The Dream Sprinkler

After their friends had left. Leanora and Rose Iris continued their journey. At sundown, as they sat by a glowing fire, there was a bright flash of light in the distance. Rose Iris ignored it, but when there was a second flash she became worried.

"Did you see the lightning? I think we are going to get a storm, Leanora. Should we try to find somewhere to shelter from the rain?" she asked.

"No, it is only Snoozlenap," the old Gypsy replied. "There's nothing to worry about. It's not going to rain tonight. He won't hurt us, he's a very gentle soul."

The flashes of light came closer and closer. Then there was a ticking sound, like that of an old clock. Only, whereas a clock says tick tock, tick tock, this sound only said tick, tick, tick, tick. It was a pleasant sound and Rose Iris began to feel quite sleepy. Suddenly she was amazed to see the most odd-looking creature appear from the trees. It kept appearing, then disappearing, with each flash of light. Coming closer and closer until eventually it appeared beside them, near the fire. The creature wasn't human, animal or insect. Although it looked like a bird, for it was covered in brightly coloured feathers, it had no wings. It had arms but there were only three fingers and a thumb on each hand. Feather-covered legs attached to feet, which had only three toes each. All this time it never stopped making a soft ticking noise through its teeth. It was much larger than Rose Iris but much smaller than Leanora. In its left hand it carried a beautiful red satin

SNOOZLENAP

bag, which it clasped tightly at the top. The bag kept wriggling and moving, as if something were trying to escape, but Snoozlenap simply clutched it tighter and tighter. Rose Iris noticed that he was sat on a floating carpet. Slowly and gently the carpet came down and spread itself softly upon the ground. Snoozlenap rested his back against an old broken fence and yawned a wide yawn.

Leanora nodded a welcome to the creature and asked if it was hungry or needed help in any way.

"Aw naw," he said, "I've been very busy tonight, delivering happy dreams to all the good children. Most of them are in bed between six o'clock and eight o'clock. I give them my best dreams. Now I have a few hours to rest before the grown-ups start going to bed. Dawnt need anything, I'm just looking forward to a good day's sleep, when I finish in the morning." The bag continued to wriggle, and Snoozlenap continued to clutch it even tighter.

"What have you got in that bag?" Rose Iris was most inquisitive.

"Aw, tis only ma dreams. Tas taken me quite a long time to share em around. What takes most of ma time, is sorting the right dream for the right person." As he spoke his eyelids kept closing and the little girl could tell that he was very tired.

"May I look inside the bag?" she asked politely.

"Ya may, but ya must be very careful not to fall in, and ya must not take too long, or ma dreams will escape," he replied.

First, he loosened the top of the bag just a little, to enable Rose Iris to peep inside. Then he lifted the little girl up between his thumb and one of the three fingers of his right hand and placed her carefully on top. When she peeped inside, she was amazed to see, swirling around and around, the most beautiful golden dust. It was like a golden whirlwind that seemed to go on and on without end. Every now and then, things popped out of the dust. A kitten, a puppy, a doll, a bicycle, a baby. They disappeared and reappeared as she watched. The swirling dust made her feel quite dizzy and she leaned further and further into the bag. If Snoozlenap had not acted very quickly, grabbing her by the foot as she began to disappear amongst the golden dust, she may have tumbled in, never to have been seen again.

"Goodness me," said Snoozlenap. "Time goes so quickly. I must start delivering the grown up's dreams, or there won't be enough time to visit them all."

He started making his tick, tick ticking noise again, which made Leanora and Rose Iris feel so tired that before long they both fell into a deep sleep. He peered into his red bag for a few seconds, then he reached in and fiddled about with the contents for a while. Pulling out a handful of golden dust, he took a small pinch of it, and sprinkled it over the tiny girl. The rest he sprinkled over Leanora. Then suddenly the fringes on the ends of the magic carpet began to wriggle. It lifted itself off the ground and with a bright flash both the carpet and Snoozlenap disappeared. Neither of the sleeping people knew he had gone. Rose Iris enjoyed a dream about her parents and little brother, whilst Leanora smiled contentedly in her sleep, as she saw visions of wonderful wild animals.

Into the Land of the Rock Trolls

At last they arrived near the rock trolls' kingdom. Toddy and his army were already there, secretly hiding in the thick bushes. In fact, they had arrived the previous day. Wind whistlers, earth crabbits, rock doppies and mud fairies were among the many creatures that accompanied him.

Rose Iris ran amongst them desperately trying to find Ilani, and she was not disappointed, for suddenly there she stood, in front of her. It was not the Ilani the little girl remembered. On her previous visit to this world, Ilani had been scatter-brained, a bit of a show-off and rarely looked neat and tidy. In front of Rose Iris now stood an elegant lady, with a neat bun on her head, and not a hair out of place. In her arms she held a baby girl, and at her side clinging to her skirt stood a young excitable boy. The mud fairy passed the baby to an earth crabbit that stood nearby, and both she and Rose Iris ran towards each other. They held each other closely for a very long time. When at last they let go of each other, the little girl saw the sadness in the mud fairy's eyes.

Leanora was impatient. There was no time to waste. Tomorrow was Queen Elvira's birthday and the present had to be prepared. She reached into the old pram, and under the blanket, which hid all her precious items from view. Pulling out a cardboard box, she emptied out the contents. Some buttons, beads, and rolls of blue, red and pink ribbon. She poked under the blanket again and pulled out four dolly pegs which she usually used to hang out her washing. Then she

ILANI, JOY AND ELRON

took a small pair of scissors from her cardigan pocket. These she used to cut four holes, one in each corner of the bottom of the box. Next, she pushed one dolly peg into each hole and put the box down upon the ground. It now stood on four legs, but it was lopsided. She straightened the pegs, so they were all the same size, then placed it down again. This time it stood perfectly level. After picking the box up once more, Leanora used the scissors to cut a small trap door, large enough for Rose Iris to pass through, where it would not be seen underneath the box when it stood on its four legs. She folded the door upwards, so it could be opened from inside the box. Next, she unrolled the pink ribbon and wrapped it neatly around the present, finishing it with a large bow. Under the bow she pierced a small hole to allow fresh air into the box. Rose Iris would be able to use the hole to peep through and see what was happening outside. The old Gypsy unpicked a fraying thread from her tatty blue cardigan and tied it around a tiny twig. This she put inside the box. Standing it carefully in one of the corners ready for use. When the time came for the little girl to creep out of the box, she would be able to throw down the thread and use it to slide to the floor.

Captain Snooty and Captain Dandy stood on the end of Toddy's nose. Behind them stood their army. They were a rather scruffy lot and their ranks were not very straight. Their lines were all wonky, and they kept pushing and shoving as they each tried to be first in line. Finally, the order was given, and they all jumped into the box. As they did so, they clumsily bumped into each other and landed on top of each other. They were a most untidy group of soldiers.

Leanora wondered if it had been the best idea to trust the

rescue to such a rubbishy army, but there was no other choice.

The old woman lifted Rose Iris, who still stood by Ilani's side, and placed her gently in the box.

It was time to finish the magic potion. Firstly, she shook the bottle five times to the right, then three times to the left, then four more times to the right. She gave it a shake up and down, before removing the cork and peeping inside. Everything was perfect. It was ready for the magical words.

"Exiglop, polygop, this magical spell
Will make rock trolls sleep, as sound as a bell.
Your chance to escape, only one hour must take,
For after that time the trolls will awake."

The bottle became teeny-tiny. Leanora passed it to Rose Iris, who waited in the box. She placed it carefully into her dress pocket. Then the old Gypsy put the lid on the box, topped it with a second bow and added some pretty yellow flowers.

"Are you all right in there" she whispered softly. "Is all well?"

"Yes, we are all well," came a chorus of voices.

"Rose Iris. If you need to put the trolls to sleep, you must pull the cork from the bottle and repeat these words. Tomalin, tustolin escobar. Do not waste the potion for there is only a small amount in the bottle."

There were two dirty, ugly rock trolls guarding the entrance to Elvira's kingdom. They were very large and extremely smelly. Luckily, they had both fallen asleep, after a boring night, sitting in the dark with nothing to do but stare into the blackness.

Leanora crept quietly forward and placed the present where they sat snoring loudly. Then she slipped silently away into the bushes to see what would happen next.

Suddenly, there was a loud noise as two more trolls marched out of the entrance to the cave to take over the watch from the sleeping guards. The two sleepers jumped to their feet and pretended that they had been awake all night. It was then that they spotted the beautiful present, tied with bright pink ribbon, and decorated with pretty yellow flowers.

All four rock trolls approached the parcel, and after thoroughly examining it, discussed what they should do. They did not think to look under the box, or they would have noticed the little trapdoor. They did, however, read the label which said, "HAPPY BIRTHDAY QUEEN ELVIRA", and decided that, since the gift was addressed to the Queen, then it belonged to the Queen. After some time, one of them lifted it up in order to present it to Her Majesty.

It was a bumpy ride. The passengers inside were thrown from one side to the other. Sometimes landing in a pile on top of each other. Rose Iris did not manage to stay on her feet, and often ended up covered in scrambling flees. It was especially unpleasant when, every now and then, the troll would tuck the box under his smelly armpit, and holding it with one hand, use a finger on the other hand to pick bogies from his nose and eat them.

Queen Elvira was walking in her gardens attended by two servants, a pretty green grasshopper and a ladybird who wore a turban, made from her favourite colour, on her head.

When Rose Iris peeped out through the tiny hole, underneath the bow, she saw the Queen jumping up and down with excitement as the trolls presented her with the wonderful gift.

Queen Elvira wore a beautiful, full-length blue gown. It had a frilly neckline and sleeves and was interwoven with pretty red flowers. Around the hemline there was a matching frill, edged with white lace, and a large bow decorated the front of the gown. On her head she wore a golden crown encrusted with large red rubies. A golden chain hung around her throat, from which glistened another large ruby, and from her ears there dangled even more of the precious stones.

"Isn't it a lovely present, Rainie?" the Queen spoke to the grasshopper. "There must be something amazing inside it. I can't wait until my birthday tomorrow."

"Yes, Your Majesty, have you seen the lovely flowers on the top?" the grasshopper replied. Then she turned to the ladybird. "Look Hazel, look at Her Majesty's adorable present. Aren't the flowers lovely? If you don't mind me saying so, Your Majesty, I am feeling a little envious."

"I love the big pink ribbon," said Hazel. "Pink is my favourite colour, you know. If Your Majesty does not want to keep the beautiful pink bows, please could I have one to make a new turban?"

Although Queen Elvira wanted to open her present immediately, she knew that she should wait until her birthday the following day, when she would open all her other presents.

"Have you checked that there is enough food for my party tomorrow?" the Queen asked.

When someone replied, "Oh yes Your Majesty. We have three nicely fatted persons," the little grasshopper's and ladybird's expressions changed from happiness to sadness.

QUEEN ELVIRA, RAINIE AND HAZEL

That evening Elvira decided to retire to her bed early, for she was feeling very tired and was impatient to see what was inside her lovely present. Everyone else was ordered to bed early also, and so the palace became silent and the lights were dimmed at an early hour.

Even the guards were ordered to their beds and everyone fell into a deep sleep. Tomorrow there would be much rejoicing and the servants would have to be up early to prepare the feast. Rainie and Hazel would be busy preparing the events. There would be acrobats, jugglers and conjurers for entertainment, and after dinner, a grand masked ball.

After it had been silent for some time, Rose Iris peeped through the little hole Leanora had made underneath the bow, once again. Nothing stirred, not even a guard or servant was awake. Captain Snooty and Captain Dandy opened the trap door and fixed the twig with the strand of wool securely across the hole. Then they threw the woollen thread out of the opening, allowing it to dangle until it reached the ground.

The flea army went first. Some climbed down the thread, but mostly they just jumped out of the hole and onto the ground. Rose Iris followed, carefully sliding down Leanora's wrinkly strand of wool, until her feet touched the floor below. Then she waited patiently for Captain Snooty and Captain Dandy to collect their troops.

The two captains tried very hard to keep their soldiers in order, but it was impossible, for they insisted on springing and bounding all over the place. After quite some time, and a great deal of fussing about, they all grouped together beneath the box.

The room was dimly lit, but they could see three doors

THE BIRTHDAY PRESENT

to exit from. Above one door hung a notice, which spelled
KITCHENS, the second read **DUNGEONS** and a third
RUBY MINES. They knew that the prisoners would not
be in the kitchens, so this left only two exits, but they did
not know which one to take. At last it was agreed that the
dungeons were the best place to start looking. So, they
crept silently through the door and stood in a long passageway. It was very dark and very smelly, but Rose Iris took
charge and led the army along until they eventually
reached a slightly better-lit area. All around the edges of
this place were cages. Some were made of iron bars. Inside
these cages stood or sat wind whistlers. They all looked
very sad and unhappy.

Cages made of trolls' hair hung from the ceiling. These
contained earth crabbits. They also looked sad and tired,
with dark shadows around their eyes. They were all as thin
as bags of bones. In the middle of the area sat four big ugly
trolls. Each of them held a large spiky club. Unfortunately,
they were all wide awake.

Rose Iris hoped she could remember the magic words for
Leanora's spell to work. She pulled and pulled until the cork
in the bottle popped out. The sound of the pop alerted the
guards. They looked around and saw the little girl and her
flea army. With a loud roar they began to tramp across the
space between themselves and the frightened intruders.

"Tomalin, tustolin escobar," Rose Iris spoke carefully and
accurately.

To her surprise, a waft of green and purple smoke came
floating out of the bottle and moved quickly towards the
trolls. It circled their heads three times before creeping up
their noses and into their ears. Almost immediately they

ROCK TROLLS, A WIND WHISTLER AND AN EARTH CRABBIT

became dizzy, swaying about in a daze, and finally falling down with very loud thumps onto the ground. Quickly, she replaced the cork in the bottle, in case she should need to use the magic potion again.

Neither Rose Iris or the army were big enough, or strong enough, to lift the keys, which hung on a chain attached to one of the trolls, so they had to think of another plan to unlock the doors of the cages. Then Captain Dandy had a very good idea.

"We must spring up into the locks and move the mechanisms, then the doors will open," he said excitedly

"What a very good plan," said Captain Snooty. So, the fleas set to work opening all the cages to allow the prisoners to escape.

They took turns, jumping up to the locks. Unfortunately, they did not always manage to reach the locks first time and had to keep trying. There were a few nasty accidents before they finally succeeded. They crept into the keyholes and worked together for once, turning the mechanisms from the inside. Then as a group they prised the doors open.

The poor creatures held captive inside the cages slowly but gradually crept nervously out of their prisons. Rose Iris walked among them, desperately, looking for Charles, Edan and Kire, but they were not amongst the hoard of skinny, starving, weary bodies.

"We will have to return to the great hall and go through the door to the mines. Captain Dandy and Captain Snooty, would you be kind enough to order your army to take these poor people back out to the entrance of the cave where Leonora and their friends and families will be waiting for them? The three of us will have to go on alone." The little girl did not want to sound too bossy. After all she did not want to upset anyone.

So, the flea soldiers took the frightened prisoners along the passageway. They headed for the tiny spot of daylight that gleamed in the distance. The two captains and Rose Iris crept silently back to the great hall and through the door with the sign above it, saying **MINES.**

This door led to a tunnel made of ice. They became extremely cold and shivery. As they breathed out, their breath almost froze. When at last they reached an opening at the other end of the tunnel they heard chip, chip, chipping sounds, mingled with loud voices, which appeared to be giving orders. Every now and then there was a sound which resembled the crack of a whip. They peered into what appeared to be a cave, and Rose Iris was amazed to see Charles and his two friends working hard, chipping rubies out of the ice. Poor Edan's and Kire's wings had been clipped short, so they could no longer fly. Guards strolled up and down and every so often would make a cracking sound with a whip and order the prisoners to work harder.

One of the rocks had a very sad, tired face. Rose Iris thought he may give them away, and alert the guards, but he said nothing. All he did was cry.

There were other prisoners in the cave who looked very skinny and weak. Charles, Edan and Kire were not at all thin.

Although looking very tired with dark circles around their eyes her friends were very plump. As a matter of fact, she had never seen them looking so podgy. Then she gave a gasp for she remembered that when asked if the food was ready for the feast, someone had said, "Yes, Your Majesty we have three plump persons."

CHARLES, EDAN AND KIRE

"Oh," she sighed, as she realised the trolls were going to eat her friends.

Her gasp alerted the guards and when they saw her, they rushed towards her, growling as they did so. The two captains moved forward to protect her, but in a flash, she removed the cork from the magic potion.

"Tomalin, tustolin escobar," she cried.

As before the green and purple smoke floated from the bottle, circled the trolls three times, then disappeared up their noses and into their ears. Their eyes began to roll around in their heads. They wibbled and they wobbled, backward and forward before falling with loud thumps onto the ground.

Rose Iris hugged her friends, but there was no time to waste. They were not sure how long it would be before the trolls would wake up. Although the magic spell said one hour, they may wake early. Quickly they headed out into the tunnel.

"Thank you," the rock called after them. "It's not nice having people chipping away at you and trying to steal your rubies. I hope the trolls will stop making people poke at me and try to take my red bits."

Charles, Edan and Kire were so plump that they found it very hard to run. The wind whistlers, earth crabbits and rock doppies were so thin and weak, that they also found it very hard to run. They moved as fast as they possibly could along the gigantic tunnel, their footsteps and voices echoed in the large open space. Along the walls, torches flickered, and threw their shadows. When the torches were behind them, their shadows looked long, dark and spooky, but as they passed under the next torch, their shadows almost disappeared.

Suddenly the way ahead split into two different ways. They panicked and discussed the problem.

"Which way shall we go?" said Captain Dandy. "Should we take the fork to the left. Or, is the fork to the right the one which will take us to the exit, and our way out from this terrible place?"

It was quickly decided to take the way to the right, but they had not gone far when they reached a dead end. So, they retraced their steps to where the cave split into two directions and followed the fork to the left. It wasn't long before they could see a small spot of daylight in the distance.

Suddenly there were loud, thumping footsteps behind them. Lots of shouting and growling.

The trolls had woken up and were coming along the tunnel. If they caught them, they would take them back to work in the ruby mines. Then, when Queen Elvira had her birthday party, they would eat Charles, Edan and Kire.

They ran as fast as they could towards the daylight and out into the open air, with the trolls close behind them.

The trolls came galloping after them, but they were filled with terror when they ran out of the tunnel and saw what awaited them. Toddy the fox, Barnie the badger, Gilliad the hare, Igywanna-the-Wise, Leanora and many other country folks. There were no trolls at all guarding the tunnel.

The trolls sunk their heels into the ground in order to stop themselves from running so quickly, but they ended up piled on top of each other on the ground. Their frightened eyes gazed at the group of creatures that stared back at them. Once they had gotten over the shock of seeing so many faces, they got to their feet and tried to run back up the tunnel.

Before they had chance to escape Leanora stepped forward and grabbed two of them by the scruff of their necks. She held them up very close to her face, which must have been terrifying for the trolls.

"Tell your Queen that if she ever sends her people out into our world again, we will all group together and catch you. We will eat you all up, even though you will most probably taste disgusting. Then Elvira will have nobody to rule over anymore," she said.

"Yes. I will gobble you up and spit you out," said Toddy.

"And I will swallow you whole and spit you out a few hours later," said Igywanna-the-Wise.

Gilliad the hare said nothing. He was too busy eating his breakfast of clover. The only other thing he did was scratch. As a matter of fact, he scratched, and he scratched, and he scratched, as he chewed, and he chewed, and he chewed.

As soon as Leanora placed the trolls back on the ground, they ran as fast as they could, back up the tunnel.

"We promise that if our Queen tries to order us to come into your world again, we will refuse to obey her, and if she insists, we will push her out of the tunnel, and you can eat her up instead of us," one of the trolls called back in a terrified voice.

"I don't think we will have to worry about rock trolls anymore," said Igywanna-the-Wise.

Ilani ran up to Charles and hugged him tightly. Then Charles lifted Elron and gave him a tight hug before taking baby Joy from her mother's arms and kissing her gently on the cheek. For the first time in a long while, the little girl smiled and made gurgling sounds in her father's arms.

GILLIAD THE HARE

Wind whistlers hugged wind whistlers, rock doppies hugged rock doppies, earth crabbits cuddled earth crabbits and mud fairies held on very tightly to each other. As a matter of fact, everyone was so excited that when they finished hugging their own folks, they all threw their arms around the other folks that were gathered together and hugged them too. Then they enjoyed a wonderful home-coming party. Some brought nuts and berries, and others collected nectar or brought homemade rose hip wine. Everyone felt sadness when they saw that the trolls had clipped off Edan's and Kire's wings. How terrible it was for them to know they would never be able to fly again.

Then, another awful thing happened. One of the wind whistlers, named Gusty, and who Rose Iris had become very friendly with, screamed in horror. He fell to his knees, desperately trying to find something that he had lost. He scratched and poked amongst the dirt and tall blades of grass.

"Oh no! I've lost it. Oh! No, no, no. Oh dear! Oh dear!" he cried. "I'll never find it in all this dirt. What will I do without one? I've had it ever since my mother gave it to me when I was born."

"Whatever is the matter? What have you lost?" Rose Iris asked.

"It's my bellybutton. I've lost my bellybutton," the poor wind whistler replied. "It was a very nice one you know, and I'll never be able to get another one."

Everyone helped Gusty to look for his bellybutton, but sadly, nobody was able to find it.

"You must have lost it in the tunnel," Rose Iris felt sorry for him, but there was nothing she could do.

Gusty walked sadly away, desperately trying to pull his vest down to cover his tummy, so nobody would see that he no longer had a bellybutton. Unfortunately, his vest was much too short and would not stretch down far enough.

Somebody Moves Home

Colleen was so happy when the fleas all came out of the tunnel. Excitedly, she ran up to Captain Snooty. She threw her arms around his neck, hugged him tightly and gave him a big kiss on the lips. Glistening tear- drops ran down over her cheeks.

"I have been so worried about you, my hero" she said, as she looked lovingly into his eyes.

Captain Dandy waited patiently for his love to come to him next, but she did not. That was when he realised that Colleen had, at last, made her choice. It was Captain Snooty whom she loved, not him. She had completely forgotten about him. With his head down, he walked sadly to where Toddy stood speaking to Leanora. As he passed Gilliad, a tiny head popped out from amongst the hare's fur. It belonged to a lady flea. Smiling prettily, she lowered her head, and fluttered her eyelashes shyly. Then the corners of her lips curled higher as she gave him the loveliest, warmest smile he had ever seen.

Captain Dandy, who did like to flirt with lady fleas, fell in love with her at once. He stood as tall and straight as a flea possibly could stand, and swaggered elegantly towards Gilliad the hare, who was still munching his breakfast of delicious pink clover. Then he jumped the highest jump he had ever jumped and landed beside the lovely lady flea. Well! you may not think a flea could be lovely, but Captain Dandy certainly did. He had already forgotten Colleen, who was still looking deeply into the adoring eyes of Captain Snooty.

"What is your name?" Captain Dandy bowed a very deep bow as he spoke. He was a perfect gentleman. Taking her hand in his, he lifted it to his lips and kissed it softly.

"I'm Edwina," she whispered sweetly. Then she continued to flutter her eyelashes and smile prettily.

"I'm Captain Dandy, and I am very pleased to meet you. I am very widely travelled you know, and have lived in Australia, Africa and a zoo in England," he boasted. "Actually, I have been living on Toddy the fox for far too long now, and it is about time I moved home again, but I don't know where to move to." He crossed his fingers behind his back, as he spoke, for he was wishing Edwina would ask him to move from Toddy the fox to Gilliad the hare.

"Well there is plenty of room on Gilliad." Edwina was most impressed by such a handsome, well-travelled stranger. "Why don't you move here?" She smiled sweetly from under her eyelashes.

That was all Captain Dandy had been waiting for. There and then he made his decision to leave his old friends and Toddy, then make new friends on Gilliad. Actually, Captain Snooty and Colleen didn't even notice that he was gone. Toddy couldn't have been happier. That was because Captain Dandy took his half of the flea army with him. The fox only had to scratch half as much as he used to, although Gilliad was forced to scratch twice as much as before.

Toddy said goodbye and walked slowly away into the bushes, looking back occasionally as he went. Gilliad sprang onto a lovely green bank and carried on eating clover, and scratching. Igywanna-the-Wise flew off into the distance and Barnie the badger shuffled off to his bed.

Leanora took her magic wand from her sleeve and pointed it towards Edan, and Kire.

"Growlio, quicklio nowlio," she said in her best witch's voice. As she spoke, a bright blue light whizzed from the end of the wand and hit the two fairies so hard that it knocked them backwards and they landed hard upon the ground. They felt a funny tingling sensation all over.

"Why have you tried to hurt us?" Kire could not believe that Leanora could be so unkind. His back was still tingling.

"I haven't tried to hurt you. Look behind you," the old Gypsy replied.

The mud fairies did as they were told and were overjoyed to see that they each had a lovely new pair of wings.

Next thing she did was magic Gusty a new bellybutton. He was so happy that he did a jig with a rock doppy called Gritty.

"May I suggest, Gusty, that in the future you wear a longer vest? You will be able to tuck it in your pants and then you will not lose your bellybutton again," Leanora advised the happy wind whistler.

"Oh! and I think you have both had enough rose hip wine," she scolded both Gusty and Gritty.

They took little notice, since they were having such a very good time.

GUSTY AND GRITTY

Having to Say Goodbye

The party continued all night long. The moon smiled down, happy to know that his moonbeams had supplied the magic dust which helped to make the magic potion. Glow worms shone their beautiful lights, and crickets provided the most wonderful music. Rose Iris recited her nursey rhymes, which made everyone laugh, but eventually the sun began to rise in the sky. Many of the folks had either fallen asleep or gone home.

Then, Oh dear! The moment Rose Iris had been dreading arrived. Leanora lifted the tiny girl up between the finger and thumb of her right hand and placed her gently into the palm of her left hand.

"I'm sorry, dear, but it is time for you to go back to the other world. I wish you could stay forever, but we both know that is not possible. Your parents will begin to worry if you are away for much longer. Although time passes much slower in the human world, I'm afraid it doesn't stand still," Leanora said sadly. "You must say goodbye now. We will miss you as much as you will miss us."

So, they all said their goodbyes. Rose Iris and Ilani hugged each other for a very long time, wishing that they did not have to say goodbye. At last they parted and Leanora lifted the little girl once more and placed her on top of the blanket in the old pram.

"Cheerio, my special friend. I hope we will meet again one day," Ilani called as she flew above the pram.

So, they travelled back to the riverbank where Rose Iris

and Leanora had met each other again, after such a long while. The little girl was sad to leave all her friends, but especially she would miss Leanora. Still she believed that one day they would see each other again.

Eventually they arrived back at the place where Rose Iris had been speaking to the tree, the stone, the dandelion and the stinging nettles. That was when it started to rain again, a light gentle shower at first, but soon the rain pelted harder and harder.

"I will miss you terribly, my little helper." Leanora gave the little girl a soft poke with her large finger as she spoke.

"We are going to see each other when I am big again. Please, Leanora, you will come and see me. Won't you?"

"I will do my best, Rose Iris, for I am sure that one day in the future I will need your help once more." As she spoke the old Gypsy reached into her pocket and pulled out the tin that contained the enchanted stones.

Now, the rain became heavier. Lightning flashed and thunder crashed at the same time, signalling that once more the storm was directly over their heads. They became wetter and wetter, until they were completely soaked to the skin.

"You know what you must do now. Touch the enchanted stones and I will say the magic words." Leanora did not want the little girl to return to the human world but she knew she had to go. "I hope we will meet again someday. I will leave you a sign so you will know that this has not been a dream," she said in a very sad voice.

Rose Iris held out her hand and touched the stones, while the old Gypsy said the same words that she always said when she was taking Rose Iris from one world to another.

"Delgora, delgora, esparto ventura.

Malafont, gorgana, alamantura."

Rose Iris felt herself growing bigger and bigger. Her clothes grew with her, but they were by now soaking wet. Her plaits hung heavy and dripping with water. At last she stopped growing, which was just as well, or she may have become a giant. She squeezed the water from her wringing wet dress. Then she glanced down at her squidgy shoes. Once more her shoelace had come undone.

"Oh dear, my lace is undone again, Leanora," she said as she bent down to re-lace it. "Leanora, what do you mean, you will leave me a sign?" She expected an answer from her friend, but none came. Standing up she looked about her and was surprised to see that the old Gypsy had gone.

"Did you see where my friend went, tree?" There was no answer from the tree either. She looked up, only to see that the tree no longer had a face. Neither did the stone, the stinging nettles or the dandelion. "I can't have dreamt all that has happened to me," she said.

Then she had an idea. She walked around to the back of the tree, and sure enough there it was. A love heart cut into the poor things back, and the letters ℬ 𝓁𝑜𝓋𝑒𝓈 ℬ beside it.

"I knew it, I knew it. It wasn't a dream." She was so excited. Then her eyes caught sight of something shining amongst the blades of grass and stinging nettles. She bent down to pick it up and was surprised to see that it was Leanora's little tin. The tin with the word "Cashews" printed on the lid. The tin the old Gypsy had kept the enchanted stones in. So that was what her friend had meant when she said, "I will leave you a sign."

As Rose Iris reached in amongst the nettles and picked up

ROSE IRIS

the tin. She remembered the warning the nettles had given her.

"We sting them and bring them up in white bumps that itch and hurt."

Very carefully, she opened up the tin and saw the three enchanted stones wrapped in pink fairy hair inside. With great care, she removed the stones with her fingertips and returned them securely into her golden locket, then tucked it safely behind the collar of her dress. How she wished Leanora had stayed a little while longer. She wanted to give her one last hug, now that she was big again. Once more the little girl had not been able to say goodbye to her dear friend.

By this time, it had stopped raining, so she placed the empty tin in her dress pocket, gave her pigtails and dress another squeeze to remove some of the water, then ran all the way home.

As she ran, she heard a very familiar voice.

"My tooe bleeeeds, Ro-sie. My tooe bleeeeds, Ro-sie. My tooe bleeeeds, Ro-sie. My tooe bleeds."

She could still hear Bert calling when at last she arrived at her garden gate.

"Oh, dear, you are absolutely soaked to the skin, sweetie," her mother said, as Rose Iris walked in through the back door. "We must get you into a nice warm bath straight away." So, the little girl had her bath, changed her clothes and enjoyed a nice cup of warm tea with two chocolate biscuits.

Before she went to sleep that night, she held her locket between her fingers. "Why didn't Leanora wait, so I could give her a big goodbye cuddle? Why couldn't I give her a hug like I did when we met at the riverbank?" she whispered.

Then she took the tin with the words Cashews out from under her pillow, where she had placed it earlier.

Suddenly she heard another voice. One which had frightened her when she heard it for the first time.

"Whoo goes there, Whoo? Whoo goes there, Whoo?"

It was Igywanna-the-Wise. Quickly she jumped out of bed and ran to the window. There he was, sat on the highest branch of a tree. He noticed her as she opened the window.

"Yoo tis yooo. Yoo tis yooo," he called.

He continued to call as she returned to her bed and tried to go to sleep. It was impossible to sleep because her head was full of all the wonderful things that had happened that day.

"Should I tell my parents about my adventure?" she whispered quietly. She thought about it for a long time, before deciding that she would not tell anybody except her best friend, who we all know was Sian, Natasha and Lana's grandmother.

Suddenly there was a familiar tick, tick, tick ticking sound. Rose Iris immediately began to feel tired and before long, she was fast asleep. She didn't see Snoozlenap sneak in through her window with his bag of pleasant dreams.

THIS REALLY IS THE END
OR, MAYBE NOT!

Lightning Source UK Ltd.
Milton Keynes UK
UKHW020726290121
377824UK00008B/135